Ian Sugarman was a primary school teacher before he began to specialise in maths. He believed that teaching maths should not only be challenging but also fun, and devised lots of practical games and puzzle activities that became popular in his home county of Shropshire and beyond. Some of these activities later became incorporated into NumberGym, a software package for schools.

More recently, he has become a volunteer reader in a local primary school, as well as a grandparent. He likes the idea that stories can open up alternative worlds to their readers.

JACK'S MAGIC PYJAMAS

IAN SUGARMAN

AUSTIN MACAULEY PUBLISHERS™

LONDON ∗ CAMBRIDGE ∗ NEW YORK ∗ SHARJAH

A CIP catalogue record for this title is available from the British Library.

ISBN 9781528997102 (Paperback)
ISBN 9781528997119 (ePub e-book)

www.austinmacauley.com

First Published (2021)
Austin Macauley Publishers Ltd
25 Canada Square
Canary Wharf
London
E14 5LQ

Dedicated to my grandson, Jack, who is a dinosaur in his spare time.

Beanstalk, who put me in contact with children who inspired me to write this story, especially Jasper.

Of course, no one knew that Jack had transformed into a rabbit.

But his parents were a bit surprised when he didn't come down for his breakfast that morning.

"Where's Jack?"
"Has he not got out of bed yet?"
"Quiet, isn't it?"

"Without him rabbiting on, you mean!"
"Oh, you're too tough on him.
He likes to talk about stuff.
You should listen to what he has to say."

Meanwhile, no one had noticed Jack as he made his way downstairs and into the garden. Luckily, the door had been left open.

He soon found himself in his mum's
vegetable patch.
He felt quite hungry.
Well, it was time for breakfast.

Strangely, he felt himself drawn to the carrots.
Now, normally, he could take them or leave them,
despite his mum saying, "Go on, have
another piece.
Carrots are so good for you."

Amazingly, with his first bite, he thought,
"That's delicious!
So he took another bite. And another. And another.

And then, to his amazement, he found himself
interested in the Brussel sprouts.
Now that's a vegetable he would never eat.
"Ummm! This is wonderful!"

Then, from the house, he could hear sounds
of panic.
"What do you mean 'he's not there'?"

"His pyjamas are lying on the bed.
Those new ones.
But there's no sign of him."

"Jack! Where are you? Jack?"

"Oh look, Mum", said Amy, Jack's sister.
"There's the prettiest bunny in the garden.
I'm going to take it upstairs."

This is all very strange, thought Jack as he nuzzled
closely to Amy's chin.
Normally, he wouldn't have anything to do with
his sister, but he found it quite comforting to be
cuddled by her.

Meanwhile, Jack's dad was considering whether he should phone the police and report a missing child.

At that moment, just as his sister had put him down on the floor, he decided he would make a bolt for it.
He dashed across the landing floor and into his own bedroom.

"Amy, leave that rabbit alone and come and help look for Jack," called his mum."

Alone in his bedroom, Jack jumped into his pyjamas.

And that's when he realised why his new pyjamas had a magic symbol on the packaging.

Because at the very moment that he touched them, he was transformed back into a boy.

Things were never quite the same after that amazing day.
He surprised his mum the next time she served Brussel sprouts.
"Yes please... are there any more?"

And he seemed to get along much better with his sister.

But, best of all, when he talked to his mum and dad, they seemed to take more interest!

THE END

9 781528 997102